Mother's Day,
El Día de las Madres

by Ana Consuelo Matiella

Illustrated by
Juana Alicia

MULTICULTURAL CELEBRATIONS II

MODERN CURRICULUM PRESS

Multicultural Celebrations was created under the auspices of
The Children's Museum, Boston.
Leslie Swartz, Director of Teacher Services,
directed this project.

Design: Gary Fujiwara
Photographs: *13*, Brian Seed/TSW;
19, 21, Robert E. Daemmrich.

MODERN CURRICULUM PRESS
13900 Prospect Road
Cleveland, Ohio 44136

ISBN 0-8136-2339-1 (soft cover) · 0-8136-2340-5 (hard cover)

3 4 5 6 7 8 9 10   98 97 96 95 94

Simon & Schuster   A Paramount Communications Company

3053900104060V

My name is Sara Moreno Gámez and I am
Mexican American. I live with my mother and father
and *Abuelita*, my mother's mother. I want to tell you
a story — a story about my whole family and a perfect
Mother's Day surprise.

Every year in May, my family has a special *fiesta* for
día de las madres, Mother's Day. All the relatives come for
a special *carne asada*, a barbecue by the river. We honor
and thank all the mothers in the family for the thoughtful
things they do for us. A mother is special —
she keeps us all strong and happy.

Chico, my cousin, is a big part of my Mother's Day story.
He is my best friend. I was born in the United States.
But Chico just moved here with *tía* Gloria, *tío* Toño,
and his brother and sister. They came from Mexico
to live near us.

Chico can play the guitar, sing, and play lots of games.
He tells me what it's like to live in Mexico. He speaks
Spanish most of the time and I speak mostly English. But
he understands English and I understand Spanish, so we
get along fine.

2

One day, Chico and I were playing with a *trompo* on the porch. My grandmother was busy sewing.

Abuelita has lived with us for three years and has taught me many things. She tries to get me to speak Spanish with her. But, I'd rather speak English like lots of my friends do. I think my mother understands this. Does *Abuelita?* I wonder...

"What are you doing, *Abuelita?*" I asked in English.

"I'm sewing a tablecloth for your mother for Mother's Day," she answered in Spanish. "If you keep working on the stitches I showed you, you'll soon be making beautiful things too," *Abuelita* added.

Chico whispered to me as he got up and left the porch. "Psst...*Sarita,ven.* Come here."

"Mother's Day is coming," he whispered. "We already made gifts for our mothers. But in Mexico, we always do something special for our grandmothers, too. Some families even hire special singers to serenade them. Let's do something special for *Abuelita* on Mother's Day!"

"Okay — let's go down to the store and buy her some talcum powder or a book!" I said.

"No, No, No!" Chico's said. "Something from the store is not good enough. It must be something we make, something special from our hearts."

6

Then his eyes brightened. "I have an idea. You know how she's always telling us we should never forget our ways and our language?" I nodded.

"I know just what we both can do to surprise her." Chico said and whispered his idea to me.

"Oh yes, that's perfect," I said. "Do you think we can be ready in time?"

"We can. We will do it together... I will teach you."

So together we worked on our Mother's Day surprise for grandmother. We practiced every day after school. It was hard and I was beginning to think a book would have been a nice gift after all.

"*Andale, Sara, yo sé que tú puedes* — Come on, Sara, I know you can do it," he told me.

"But will I be able to do it in time?" I thought to myself.

9

The day before the *carne asada, Abuelita* was making *flores de papel* – paper flowers, with my mother.

"Come," Grandmother said to us in Spanish. "I can show you how. Always put a little drop of vanilla in the center of each one. It makes them smell so sweet."

"And they are sweeter because you have learned to make them from your grandmother," my mother added.

Chico and I worked hard. When the flowers were finished, we filled a *piñata* with them. The *piñata* was shaped like a basket of flowers. The other cousins would be so excited.

Finally, Mother's Day arrived. Everyone helped get ready for the celebration. The long wooden tables covered with colorful cloths were set up by the river. Paper streamers and the piñata were strung between the giant cottonwood trees.

The *comal* was ready for the *tías* to make *tortillas*. The *tíos* started to grill meat and prepare fresh green chiles for the *salsa fresca*. Delicious smells filled the air and everyone was happy.

After we had eaten, Chico came running. "It's time. It's time, Sara! *Tío* Toño will announce us."

"Atención! Atención!" *Tío* Toño yelled loudly. "Chico and Sara have a surprise gift for one very special mother!"

Chico winked at me. We were ready. We waited for everyone to be quiet. Then we came out from behind a tree singing *Las mañanitas.* We walked slowly to where *Abuelita* was sitting.

I knew the minute we started the first verse it was going to be all right. I was singing...I was singing in Spanish!

El día que tu naciste, nacieron todas las flores.
El día que tu naciste, cantaron los ruiseñores.
Despierta mi bien. Despierta.
Mira que ya amaneció Ya los pajaritos cantan.
La luna ya se metió

In English it means:
On the day you were born, all the flowers were
born too.
On the day you were born, all the nightingales sang.
Wake up, my dear. Wake up.
Look, the sun is coming up.
Already the birds are singing and
The moon has gone away.

18

Las Mañanitas is a song we sing to tell someone they are special.

After we finished the song, everyone clapped and cheered. They were glad we had sung this song to *Abuelita,* our family treasure.

Abuelita said to me in Spanish. "Your gift was very, very special. I am so happy to hear you sing in our language."

"I am happy, too, *Abuelita,*" I answered. "I never knew how happy and proud I would feel to sing in Spanish."

Then we children broke the piñata. As the empty piñata swung back and forth the *flores de papel* that we had made spilled everywhere. And everything smelled sweet, like vanilla.

Glossary

Abuelita (ah-bway-LEE-tuh) grandmother

carne asada (CAHR-nuh ah-Sah-duh) barbeque, or to grill meat

comal (koh-MAHL) a flat grill used to cook tortillas

flores de papel (FLOH-rehs deh pah-PEHL) paper flowers

piñata (pee-NYAH-tuh) a large shape made of paste and paper that is filled with candy or flowers

salsa fresca (SAHL-sah FREHS-kuh) a sauce or relish made of fresh onions, tomatoes, green chiles, and cilantro

tía (TEEUH) aunt

tío (TEEOH) uncle

tortilla (tohr-TEE-uh) a flat round pancake made of either corn or wheat flour

trompo (TROMPoh) a Mexican toy, a spinning top

About the Author

Ana Consuelo Matiella was born in Nogales, Sonora, Mexico, and immigrated to the United States when she was 7 years old. She is a mother, an aunt, a writer and an editor. Ms. Matiella has written a great deal about multicultural education. She lives in Sante Fe, New Mexico with her husband, daughter, two dogs and one guinea pig.

About the Illustrator

Juana Alicia has painted murals for 10 years, creating works in San Francisco, and Nicaragua. She received her MFA at the San Francisco Art Institute. She has taught at Stanford, the University of California, and California College of Arts and Crafts. She now works with the art for social change program at New College of California in San Francisco. She lives there with her husband, artist, Emmanuel Montoya and two children, Justine and Mayahuel.